Stormy Weather?
Stick Together!

by Suzy Spafford

Level **1** Reader

Splash!

"Don't get me wet, Suzy!" said Emily Marmot.

"Why not?" asked her brother, Ollie.

"The wetter, the better!"

Suzy just giggled. "Come on," she said,

"we're almost at Grandma Gussie's garden shed."

What a cozy place! They were just
in time for the two o'clock meeting
of the Duckport Adventure Club.
Corky rushed in behind them.
"I thought I was going to blow away
out there!" he cried.

The wind blew.

"Where's Jack?" asked Suzy.

"He should be here by now."

Thunder boomed far away.

"Oh, my!" said Emily.

"I hope Jack is okay."

Grandma Gussie came to the door.

"Cookies!" she said with a smile.

"Jack is not here yet," said Suzy.

"Where could he be?"

"Oh, I think Jack is just fine,"

Grandma Gussie said.

"He's only five minutes late.

He often loses track of the time."

"But he's out in the storm!" cried Emily.
"It's cold. And wet! And scary!"

"Not for a duck like Jack," said Grandma
Gussie. "In fact, it was because of a storm
that our town of Duckport began."

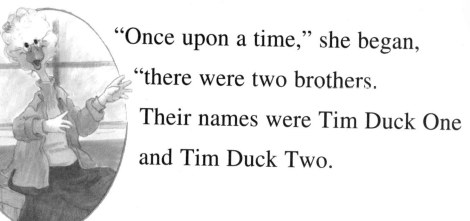

"Once upon a time," she began,
"there were two brothers.
Their names were Tim Duck One
and Tim Duck Two.

"It was time for their flock to fly
to Alaska for the summer. But the
brothers lost track of the time.
The flock left without them!

"So Tim Duck One and Tim Duck Two
set out on their own. Well, they flew right
into a storm! They couldn't see!
They were lost!

"When the storm was over, they looked down.

They were not over Alaska.

But they did see some islands.

"It was a wonderful place!
'I must find my way
to Alaska,'
said Tim Duck Two.
'I must tell all the
other ducks about this
place.'

"And that is exactly what he did!
All the ducks stuck together and built
the town of Duckport. And it was because
of two ducks who lost track of the time—
and a big storm!"

Suddenly, Jack burst in.

"Sorry I'm late!" he said.

"Where were you?" asked Suzy.

"I lost track of the time, I guess," Jack said.

That made everyone laugh.

"Now," Grandma Gussie said,
"what shall we do together?"
"Tell ghost stories!" yelled Jack.

Corky went first.

"Once upon a time," he said, "there
was a boy lost in a cave!
It was filled with big,
hairy spiders."

"Eeeuuww!" said Emily.

"What happened?"

"He turned into Rocket Turtle,"
Corky said, "and escaped!"

Emily went next.

"A girl got a fancy tea set
for her birthday. And she did *not*
write a thank-you note. The end."

"That was your scary story?"

Jack asked.

"Of course!" said Emily.

"Bad manners are *very frightening*!"

Jack and Suzy told a scary joke together.
"What should you do if a monster runs
in the front door?" asked Jack.

"Run out the back door!"
cried Suzy.
Ollie laughed so hard,
he got the hiccups.

"Rainy days can be fun," Emily said.
"Yes," said Suzy. "As long as we're
together—inside where it's warm and dry!"